Here you go
Buckaroo

Love ya
Pop Pop
&
Naana

XMAS 2013   XOXO

COWBOY SAM
AND THOSE CONFOUNDED
SECRETS

WRITTEN BY **KITTY GRIFFIN** AND **KATHY COMBS**

ILLUSTRATED BY **MIKE WOHNOUTKA**

CLARION BOOKS · NEW YORK

Clarion Books
a Houghton Mifflin Company imprint
215 Park Avenue South, New York, NY 10003
Text copyright © 2001 by Kitty Griffin and Kathy Combs
Illustrations copyright © 2001 by Mike Wohnoutka

The illustrations were executed in acrylic on watercolor paper.
The text was set in 16-point Garamond Book Condensed.

For information about permission to reproduce selections from this book,
write to Permissions, Houghton Mifflin Company, 215 Park Avenue South, New York, NY 10003.

www.houghtonmifflinbooks.com

Printed in Singapore.

Library of Congress Cataloging-in-Publication Data

Griffin, Kitty.
Cowboy Sam and those confounded secrets / by Kitty Griffin and Kathy Combs ; pictures by Mike Wohnoutka.
p. cm.
ISBN 0-618-08854-7
[1. Secrets—Fiction. 2. West (U.S.)—Fiction. 3. Humorous stories.]
I. Combs, Kathy. II. Wohnoutka, Mike, ill. III. Title.
PZ7.G881358 Co 2001
[E]—dc21
00-065733

TWP 10 9 8 7 6
4500213020

In memory of Ian and Jan
—K.G. and K.C.

To my family
—M.W.

ight could be Cowboy Sam was the most favorite man in the whole town of Dry Gulch.

It wasn't just 'cause Cowboy Sam was smart. Whoa, doggies, that Sam was smart—smart as an armadillo rootin' up insects in the dark.

It wasn't just 'cause Cowboy Sam was tough. Whoa, doggies, that Sam was tough—tough as a longhorn's horns.

And it wasn't just 'cause Cowboy Sam was kind. Whoa, doggies, that Sam was kind—kind as the shade of a pecan tree on a hot summer's day.

It was 'cause Cowboy Sam could be depended on to keep a secret. Whenever anyone asked him, "Sam, can you keep a secret?" Sam replied in his slow Texas drawl, "I'll keep it under my hat." And so he did.

Under Cowboy Sam's hat were more secrets than fleas on Doc Peeble's hound dog (and that's a whole lot of fleas).

More secrets than peppers on a chili pepper plant (and that's a whole lot of peppers).

More secrets than spikes on a horny toad (and that's a whole lot of spikes).

Every Saturday when Sam rode into town to get supplies, the townspeople were itchin' to tell him secrets.

One particular Saturday, something downright peculiar occurred.
The day started out as normal as a blue jay soaring through the blue skies.

"Morning, Sam," called out Levi the leather goods dealer. "Can I talk to you?"

Sam nodded and moseyed across the street to Levi's Leather Goods Shop. Levi whispered something in Sam's ear and then added, "Shhh. Don't forget. It's a secret."

Sam nodded and said what he always said, "I'll keep it under my hat."

As Sam went about his shopping, Miss Fannie the feed store owner had a secret, and so did Burley the blacksmith. Cowboy Sam listened politely and said what he always said, "I'll keep it under my hat."

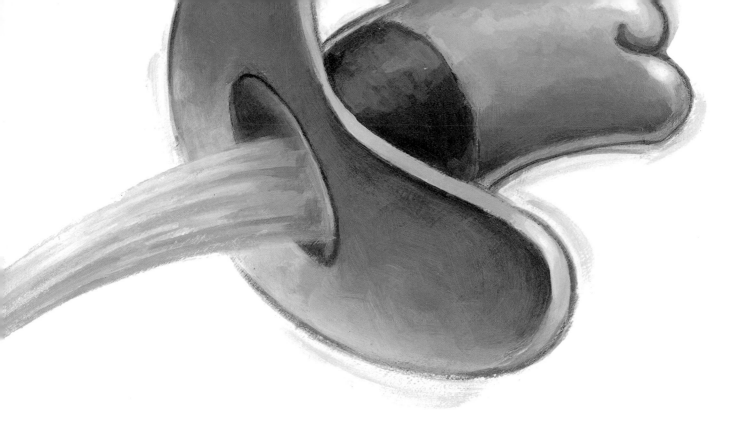

When Sam got to the end of town, the most confounded thing happened. Parson Perkins called out to him, "Can I tell you a secret?" But before Sam could nod his usual nod, his hat popped clean off his head.

The townspeople all stopped and stared. Sam snatched up his hat, put it back on his head, and started walking.

By the time he got back to Burley's Blacksmith Shop, that hat had popped off again, higher than a jackrabbit jumping over a prickly pear cactus.

Sam took ahold of that hat and put it back on his head. But it wouldn't stay put.

No one knew what to do or say. Little Leroy ran over and peered inside Sam's hat. "It's got too many secrets in it," he declared.

Sam wiped his brow. "That just can't be," he said. But try as he might, the hat would not stay on his head.

The townspeople grumbled. What would happen to all their secrets?

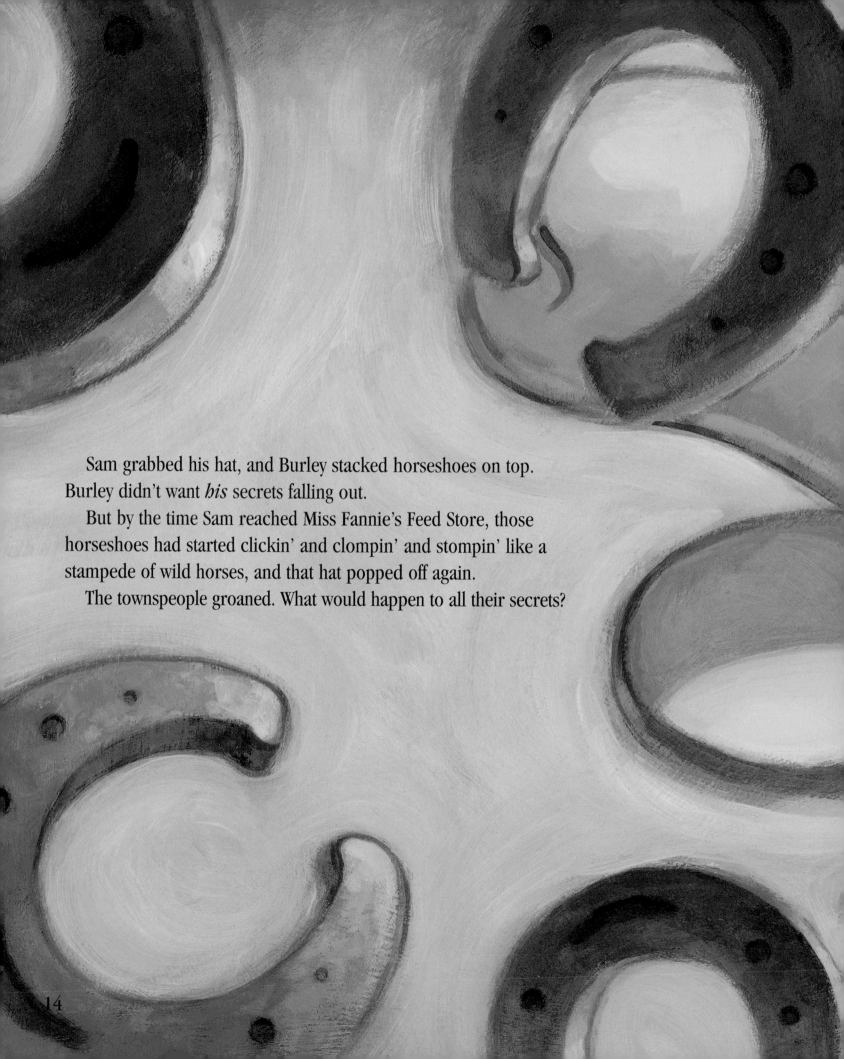

Sam grabbed his hat, and Burley stacked horseshoes on top. Burley didn't want *his* secrets falling out.

But by the time Sam reached Miss Fannie's Feed Store, those horseshoes had started clickin' and clompin' and stompin' like a stampede of wild horses, and that hat popped off again.

The townspeople groaned. What would happen to all their secrets?

Sam held his hat by the brim, and Miss Fannie hoisted a 25-pound bag of oats on top. Miss Fannie didn't want *her* secrets falling out.

But by the time Sam reached Levi's Leather Goods Shop, that hat had twitched and twittered so much that the oat bag burst, and oats poured down like a Texas thunderstorm. And off flew Sam's hat again.

The townspeople gasped. What would happen to all their secrets?

Sam clutched the brim once again, and Levi tied it down with a leather strap. Levi sure didn't want *his* secrets falling out.

Sam started walking. That hat began to bounce. It squirmed. It pulled on the strap. It pulled so hard that Sam coughed and choked. Quickly he untied the knot. That hat blasted off and shot up in the air, where it hung for a second, then started to drop. Secrets tumbled out everywhere.

The townspeople scattered like marbles. No one wanted to be there with all those runaway secrets.

19

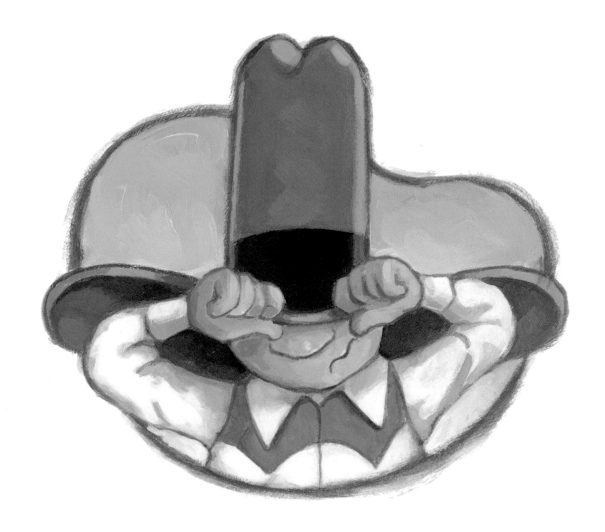

Cowboy Sam quickly gathered up the secrets and stuffed them back in his hat.

Not being one to give in, he decided to try one more thing. He pulled that hat down tight. Then, quick as you can pick a cotton boll, Sam flipped over and stood on his head.

Finally, he had that hat.

But not for long.

That hat squirmed. That hat bucked. That hat exploded and blew Sam way up into the air like a wild turkey. All the secrets rocketed into outer space. Sam came down through the roof of Herman's Hat Shop.

Cowboy Sam was all tuckered out. He looked sadly at the huge hole in his hat.

"That hat won't be keeping the rain off your head," said Herman.

"Nope," replied Sam.

"And it won't be keeping any more secrets in," said Herman.

"Nope," replied Sam.

"And you know," said Herman, "this town's liable to go plum crazy without a secret-keeper."

"Yep," replied Sam.

"Especially me," said Herman. "I had one whopper of a secret to tell you, Sam."

Sam picked up his hat, climbed up on his horse, and headed home.

He had let everybody down.

He felt more bamboozled than an armadillo without his armor.

More dejected than a crawdad without his craw.

More lonesome than a Texas Ranger without his range.

Sam sighed a sigh as deep as Palo Duro Canyon and sat on his porch like a lump of cold grits. That's where Sheriff Sherman and the rest of the townspeople found him. They came in a convoy, toting gifts for Sam to keep his secrets in.

Levi brought him a saddlebag—but it was too much trouble to get all those straps undone.

Miss Fannie brought him a shopping basket—but it had holes in it.

Burley brought him a big iron box—but it was too heavy to tote around.

Herman brought him the biggest hat anybody had ever seen—but it slid down over Sam's eyes.

Then Little Leroy marched right up to Sam carrying a homemade cherry pie.

Sam just shook his head and said, "Little Leroy, I can't keep secrets in a pie!"

"Gosh, Sam, it ain't for keepin' secrets in," said Little Leroy. "Granny Grams told me to bring this to you to make you feel better. You know she's got a heart as big as Texas."

Everyone nodded in agreement.

"That's it!" shouted Sam. He jumped up and down and his spurs jingled and jangled. "Yippity-skippity, that's it!" Sam danced with Miss Fannie. "Yee-haw!"

It was obvious to the townspeople that he had an idea.

"Who has a secret to tell me?" Sam asked, eyeballing the crowd.

"Where are you going to keep it?" Burley asked.

"Who's got a secret?" Sam asked again, ignoring Burley's question.

Herman was bustin' at the seams. He hustled forward and whispered into Sam's ear. Sam nodded and said out loud in his slow Texas drawl, "I'll hold it . . . in my heart."

The townspeople whooped and hollered. They threw their hats in the air.

Then, out of the crowd stepped tight-lipped Tessa. A hush fell all around. The townspeople gawked. Would she really tell a secret?

Tessa paid no attention to the crowd. She looked straight into Cowboy Sam's eyes and said, "I never trusted that hat, Sam, but I do trust your heart." Then she leaned close and whispered in his ear.

Sam nodded and replied in his slow Texas drawl, "I'll hold it in my heart."

And so he did.